ABOUT THE BANK STREET READY-TO-READ SERIES

Seventy years of educational research and innovative teaching have given the Bank Street College of Education the reputation as America's most trusted name in early childhood education.

Because no two children are exactly alike in their development, we have designed the *Bank Street Ready-to-Read* series in three levels to accommodate the individual stages of reading readiness of children ages four through eight.

- *Level 1:* GETTING READY TO READ—read-alouds for children who are taking their first steps toward reading.
- *Level 2:* READING TOGETHER—for children who are just beginning to read by themselves but may need a little help.
- *Level 3:* I CAN READ IT MYSELF—for children who can read independently.

Our three levels make it easy to select the books most appropriate for a child's development and enable him or her to grow with the series step by step. The *Bank Street Ready-to-Read* books also overlap and reinforce each other, further encouraging the reading process.

We feel that making reading fun and enjoyable is the single most important thing that you can do to help children become good readers. And we hope you'll be a part of Bank Street's long tradition of learning through sharing.

The Bank Street
College of Education

For Molly Elizabeth Davies
—W.H.H.

To my niece and nephew, Laura and David,
and Rocco the cat,
the dizziest dog I know
—G.B.

A DOZEN DIZZY DOGS
A Bantam Little Rooster Book
Simultaneous paper-over-board and trade paper editions/September 1990

Little Rooster is a trademark of Bantam Books,
a division of Bantam Doubleday Dell Publishing Group, Inc.

Series graphic design by Alex Jay/Studio J
Associate Editor: Gillian Bucky

Special thanks to James A. Levine, Betsy Gould,
Erin B. Gathrid, and Gwendolyn Dunaif.

Library of Congress Cataloging-in-Publication Data

Hooks, William H.
A dozen dizzy dogs / William H. Hooks ;
illustrated by Gary Baseman.
p. cm. — (Bank Street ready-to-read)
"A Byron Preiss book."
"A Bantam little rooster book."
Summary: A dozen dizzy dogs have
an adventure with a bone.
ISBN 0-553-05892-4. — ISBN 0-553-34923-6 (pbk.)
[1. Dogs—Fiction. 2. Stories in rhyme.
3. Counting.]
I. Baseman, Gary, ill. II. Title. III. Series.
PZ8.3.H765Do 1990
[E]—dc20

89-18303 CIP AC

Published simultaneously in the United States and Canada

Bantam Books are published by Bantam Books, a division of Bantam Doubleday Dell Publishing Group, Inc. Its trademark, consisting of the words "Bantam Books" and the portrayal of a rooster, is Registered in U.S. Patent and Trademark Office and in other countries. Marca Registrada. Bantam Books, 666 Fifth Avenue, New York, New York 10103.

PRINTED IN THE UNITED STATES OF AMERICA

0 9 8 7 6 5 4 3 2

Bank Street Ready-to-Read™

A Dozen Dizzy Dogs

by William H. Hooks
Illustrated by Gary Baseman

A Byron Preiss Book

A BANTAM LITTLE ROOSTER BOOK

NEW YORK • TORONTO • LONDON • SYDNEY • AUCKLAND

ONE dizzy dog,
digging all alone.

TWO dizzy dogs,
digging up a bone.

THREE dizzy dogs,
scratching with their claws.

FOUR dizzy dogs,
pulling with their paws.

FIVE dizzy dogs,
loading up their prize.

SIX dizzy dogs,
flying through the skies.

SEVEN dizzy dogs,
landing with a groan.

CRACK!

EIGHT dizzy dogs,
picking up the bone.

NINE dizzy dogs,
making a repair.

TEN dizzy dogs,
rushing to the fair.

ELEVEN dizzy dogs,
entering their prize.

CONTEST

1ST
PRIZE

TWELVE dizzy dogs,
can't believe their eyes!

ELEVEN dizzy dogs,
singing, "Arf, we won!"

TEN dizzy dogs,
dancing in the sun.

NINE dizzy dogs,
dividing up the bone.

EIGHT dizzy dogs,
starting out for home.

SEVEN dizzy dogs,
riding on a train.

SIX dizzy dogs,
running through the rain.

FIVE dizzy dogs,
swimming through a flood.

FOUR dizzy dogs,
slipping in the mud.

THREE dizzy dogs,
racing to their homes.

TWO dizzy dogs,
hiding their big bones.

ONE dizzy dog,
digging once again!

William H. Hooks is the author of many books for children, including the highly-acclaimed *Moss Gown* and, most recently, *The Three Little Pigs and the Fox.* He is also the Director of Publications at Bank Street College. As part of Bank Street's Media Group, he has been closely involved with such projects as the well-known Bank Street Readers and Discoveries: An Individualized Reading Program. Mr. Hooks lives with three cats in a Greenwich Village brownstone in New York City.

Gary Baseman is an award-winning illustrator whose work can be seen in *Time* magazine, *The Atlantic, Discover,* and *Sports Illustrated,* among other publications. He has also written and designed animation for television. Born and raised in Los Angeles, Mr. Baseman now calls Brooklyn, New York, home.